GINGER

DOG DIARIES

#1: GINGER

#2: BUDDY

DOG DIARIES

GINGER

BY KATE KLIMO • ILLUSTRATED BY TIM JESSELL

Random House 🏠 New York

With thanks to Stephen L. Zawistowski, Ph.D., CAAB, Adjunct
Professor of Clinical Medicine, University of Illinois College of
Veterinary Medicine, for his assistance in the preparation of this book.

Visit us on the Web! randomhouse.com/kids

Educators and librarians, for a variety of teaching tools, visit us at
RHTeachersLibrarians.com

Library of Congress Cataloging-in-Publication Data
Klimo, Kate.
Ginger / Kate Klimo ; illustrated by Tim Jessell. — 1st ed.
p. cm.
Summary: Ginger the golden retriever narrates the story of her life, from her birth in a puppy
mill through the various people who have "owned" her.
Includes bibliographical references.
ISBN 978-0-307-97899-8 (trade) — ISBN 978-0-307-97901-8 (lib. bdg.) —
ISBN 978-0-307-97902-5 (ebook)
1. Golden retriever—Juvenile fiction. [1. Golden retriever—Fiction. 2. Dogs—Fiction.]
I. Jessell, Tim, ill. II. Title.
PZ10.3.W927Gi 2013 [Fic]—dc23 2012004127

Printed in the United States of America

10 9 8 7 6 5 4 3 2 1

First Edition

To George, wherever you are,

with love from your once and *furever* mom

—K.K.

CONTENTS

PUPPY NUMBER ONE OF SIX

My name is Ginger. I'm a golden retriever, and this is my story. Ginger wasn't always my name. In the beginning, I was Puppy Number One of Six, Batch Three, Cage Nine. Ginger came later, along with lots of adventures—some good, some bad—which I'll tell you about if you like.

When I first came into this world, I was blind and deaf. I remember Mother's Milk, sweet and warm. And I remember her big, rough tongue washing over me, waking up my tiny body to all the things it could do: eat and see and hear and sniff and yawn and scratch and wag and poop. I remember Mother's smell: Milk and Fur and Heat.

I remember my brothers and sisters. There were six of us in all, three females and three males, all crowded together in a wire cage barely big enough for Mother to stand up in. It was small and cramped and the wire cut into the tender pads of our feet, but it was the whole world to us. On the other side of the wire, there were other dogs and puppies in cages of their own, but they were too far away for us to talk to them. Our sky was the roof of an old barn with so many holes in it, the rain and snow got in.

A female, I was the firstborn, and the biggest and strongest of the litter. I was also the first one to discover Play. As far back as I can remember, I loved Play. Even during my darkest days, I have always been on the lookout for fun.

I was only fourteen days old when I first squirmed up to my brother. *Hey!* I said, as I grabbed his floppy ear in my mouth and tugged with all my might.

Hey yourself! Floppy Ears replied, boxing me in the eye with a big, soft paw.

Oh, yeah? I said, clamping my toothless mouth over his muzzle.

Yeah! he said, shaking me off and fastening his mouth over mine. And then we were at it: all ears and tails and bellies, rolling and tussling and yapping and having a fine old time, until Mother put her big, wet nose between us and said, *That's enough fooling around.*

But did we listen? No, we did not. We were having too much fun. Mother growled low in her

throat and glared at us. We froze, then fell away from each other. To this very day, when a two-legger glares at me, I'm a pup all over again, being scolded by Mother. My head hangs down, my tail goes between my legs, and I stop whatever it is that I'm doing.

I felt bad until Mother tucked me against her warm side. I latched on to her nipple and sucked hard to bring that wonderful, sweet milk squirting into my mouth. If I had known what was coming, I would have helped myself to twice as much. But we never know what's coming, do we?

"Little Golden Nuggets," Old Farmer called us. I don't know what he meant by that, but it wasn't anything good. He was a big two-legger with rough hands and a gruff voice, and he smelled like Meat and Smoke. Whenever he opened the cage to fill Mother's bowl with mush, she cowered and whimpered.

The rest of the time, when Old Farmer wasn't around, Mother was okay. But she was always tired. She never had time for Play. As we got bigger, we learned to amuse ourselves. We played Chase the Tail and Shake the Rag and Knock Over the Bowl.

After we wore each other out, we would fall asleep in a big heap with me always on top. I kept the smaller ones toasty underneath me. It got cold in the cage, and Mother didn't want us suckling all the time. In the end, though, tired as she was, she always brought us back close to her. I think she worried about us less when we were there.

I don't remember when she started putting all her worry on Little Bit. While the rest of us kept growing, Little Bit seemed to be shrinking. When the rest of us were nursing, Little Bit would just sit there with her eyes closed or wander off. Milk didn't seem to interest her. Mother kept bringing her back, but Little Bit kept going off on her own.

One day, Little Bit crawled over to the far side of Mother's feed bowl and wouldn't come back. We called to her, *Little Bit! Come play!* But she didn't answer. At first, we thought she might have gotten her paw stuck in the cage. That happened to us sometimes. It hurt to be trapped like that! Thinking she might need my help, I went over and grabbed hold of her ear and tugged, but she wouldn't move. She just lay there, small and cool and still.

Mother picked her up, but Little Bit wouldn't lift her head or open her eyes. Mother licked her and licked her, but she couldn't lick the life back into Little Bit. So Mother shoved her away with her nose, then went back to her usual spot in the corner of the cage. She circled three times, like she always did, and then lay down. She let out a gusty sigh.

The rest of us whined, *What's wrong? What's wrong with Little Bit, Mother?*

Puppies, she told us, *your sister is dead.*

Dead? we said. *What's that?* What did we know

of death, us puppies, who were squirming and wagging and pouncing with life?

It means she went over the Rainbow Bridge. She won't ever nurse or play or grow up to be a big dog like the rest of you will, if you eat your food, mind your manners, and do what you're told.

Oh, we said. We lost no time going back to suckling and resolved to be good little puppies.

Meanwhile, Mother lay back and said, *I'm so tired! Too many pups in too little time, and me barely more than a pup myself.*

It wasn't long after this that Old Farmer came. He opened the cage and scooped up Little Bit. Before he took her away, he said to Mother, "Lost Number Six, did you? Well, it looks like the other five of your little nuggets are almost ready to cash in."

Mother pulled back into the corner of the cage

and gathered us to her. After that, she began to feed us in a different way. She would gobble up the food in her bowl and mix it with her spit until it was warm and soupy. Then she would force it down our throats. It didn't taste anywhere near as sweet and good as her milk. My brothers and sister spat it out, but I swallowed it all and opened my mouth and asked for more. After a while, the others caught on and did the same. A week or so after we started eating food this way, when we were eight weeks old, Old Farmer came and took Mother away.

At first, we thought he was going to bring her back and maybe bring back Little Bit, too. We waited at the front of the cage, our damp little muzzles pressed to the wire. When Mother didn't come, we began to call out for her.

Mama! Mama! Mama!

It got dark. Without Mother's big, warm body, we were chilled to the bone. We slept where we stood.

Finally, I went over to the place where Mother usually lay. I turned around three times and curled up nose to tail. Floppy Ears joined me.

I miss Mother, he said.

Me too, I said with a sigh.

Then the other three snuggled in beside us. We slept in a pile, the smell of Milk and Fur and Heat already beginning to fade. In the night, I woke up and sniffed around, taking in every bit of Mother's scent. I knew then that this would be the last of her I would ever sniff.

2

How Much Is That Doggie
in the Window?

In the morning, Old Farmer filled the bowl with mush. "Eat up, Nuggets!" he told us. "You've got a long trip ahead of you."

I didn't understand him, but I ate the cold mush and made sure that my brothers and sister did, too. Floppy Ears ate so fast that he puked it up. Then he gobbled up the puke and licked his chops. I didn't hold it against him. It probably tasted like Mother had chewed it for him first.

Poor Floppy Ears!

Poor us!

That afternoon, Old Farmer picked up Cage Nine, sending us tumbling into one corner. No sooner did we find our legs than the cage tilted again and we tumbled to the other side. Farmer carried us to the mouth of a great stinky black box on wheels and set Cage Nine down with a rude *bump* that rattled the brains in our heads. Later, I learned this box on wheels was called a Truck. When I got bigger and was on the loose, I chased Trucks whenever I got the chance. It was my little way of getting back at them for what this one did to us.

The Truck rumbled and heaved all over the place. Cage Nine slid from side to side and back and forth. We scrambled to keep our footing but

always seemed to wind up in a heap in one corner, stumbling and stepping on each other's heads. It was like being a newborn all over again, helpless and clumsy, only without Mother there to set us right.

Even though it was dark in the back of the Truck, I could smell that we weren't alone. Once my eyes got used to the darkness, I saw that the Truck was filled with other cages just like ours. There were stacks and stacks of cages filled with puppies of all shapes and sizes. There were puppies above us and puppies below us and puppies all around us. All of us were piddling and pooping and puking and yipping and yapping and tumbling into heaps as the truck rumbled along. We all smelled the same. We smelled like Fear. And we all called out the same questions, over and over:

Where are we going?

Mama? Mama? Mama?

We yelled until our throats were raw, and then we fell into an exhausted sleep.

Suddenly, the Truck stopped moving. The back wall thundered open and light blazed in. I blinked and sat up. A female two-legger climbed into the truck and put her face close to our cage.

"Aren't you a cute little batch of goldies?" she said in a soft voice. "But *pee-yew*! You little guys need a bath!"

I didn't know what she meant, but I knew it wasn't good. My littermates and I were dumped out of our cage. Our Fear grew! First, we lost Mother, and now we were losing Cage Nine.

Next, we were put into a big bowl, much bigger than our food dish. We tried to climb out of it, but it was too steep and slippery. Water came gushing into the bowl. White foam started billowing everywhere. It tasted terrible! It smelled like

Sadness and Wet Fur and something else I would later learn was called Flea Bath. Even when I became an old dog, I would run from the words Flea Bath. Why two-leggers think Flea Bath is necessary is a mystery to me. I shook and sneezed. Then the female two-legger picked me up and rubbed me dry. She rubbed me for extra long just behind my ears, and it felt so good it made my hind leg go *thump-thump-thump.*

"You like that, don't you, Puppy Number One?" she crooned in my ear.

Like it? I turned my head and gave her a big, wet swipe of my tongue.

"You're a kisser, too," she said. "I wish I could take you home, but my mother says no more dogs. Let's hope you and your brothers and sister go to a good home."

I didn't know what she meant, but I liked her

so much I licked her again. She tasted salty and sour at the same time. She smelled like Dog and Flea Bath.

The new world we found ourselves in was a big, bright, shiny room with fragrant shavings on the floor. At first, I just stood there. I couldn't smell myself. The Flea Bath had robbed me of something important: the Scent of Me. I couldn't smell my brothers and sister, either, so I was very upset. Then I got an idea. I squatted and piddled and rolled in it a little, and before long, I smelled much better. My old self again! The Scent of Me was back!

But this new world was strange. The floor was slippery. The walls were slippery, too, and I could see right through one of them. On the other side of the Invisible Wall were more two-leggers than I had ever seen. All shapes and sizes of them were coming up and tapping on the wall and pressing their muzzles and their paws to it.

My brothers and sister huddled in a corner.

I bounded over to them. *Hey, guys!* I called out. *Remember Play? Let's have some fun!*

But those puppy party poopers just dug deeper into their furry heap.

Floppy Ears peered at me from behind one ear. *Shhh. If they think we're sleeping, maybe they'll go away and leave us alone.*

But this was no time to hide and pretend to sleep! For all I knew, Mother might be somewhere out there, beyond the Invisible Wall. How could I get past it and see for myself?

Suddenly, a little head popped up on the other side of the Invisible Wall. I could tell by this two-legger's size that he wasn't much more than a puppy himself. He put his hands up and smeared the wall with something that looked tasty. I licked

at the smear, but I couldn't taste a thing. I pounded my fists against the Invisible Wall.

Help! Help! Let me out! I shouted, panting from the effort. Then I slid down the wall and stared up at my new friend with Sad Eyes.

The two-legger grinned and pressed his chubby pink face up against the Invisible Wall. I leapt up and licked him. He pulled back and squealed and giggled.

The big two-leggers on either side of him pointed to me. The little one jumped up and down and squealed some more.

I wasn't sure what was going on. I did know that this human pack had chosen me for something. I immediately liked them. I didn't know what was coming next, but I knew that I would do anything—*anything in the world*—to please them.

GINGERBREAD

I had never felt so alone as I did that first night after leaving the Invisible Wall room. Mother was gone, Cage Nine was gone, and now so were my littermates. I was all alone in a box not much bigger than I was. There were holes in its side, and if I peered very hard through them, I could see that I was surrounded by the things that two-leggers wear on their feet, which I later learned are called

Shoes. I don't chew Shoes anymore because I know better, but back then? I loved Shoes. I liked the way they smelled. I liked the way they tasted. At that moment, I had never chewed a single Shoe and yet somehow I knew I was meant to. I longed to get out of the box and sink my teeth into one. Just looking at those things made my mouth water and the sharp teeth that were working their way through my gums tingle.

Every so often, one of the big two-leggers who had chosen me would open the box and pat me on the head or drop in some food or set down a small bowl of water. I liked the pats, but I was too nervous to drink or eat.

The female told me, "Be patient, little girl. You're Dylan's big surprise."

She didn't smell like my mother, but she smelled like *somebody's* mother. She was Dylan's Mother.

And her voice was kind, so I yawned and licked my lips and tried very hard not to worry.

Later, the man opened the box and stroked my head and let me lick his hand. Oh, how yummy and sweet it tasted! I found delicious crumbs hiding between his fingers, and I snaked my tongue between them and licked up every last crumb. Then I thumped my tail against the side of the box because I wanted more, more, more!

"You like that, huh, girl?" Yummy Crumb Man said to me.

I wagged my tail and made Sad Eyes.

"Those are gingerbread crumbs!" he said. "Hey, that's what we'll call you—Ginger! Dylan's going to be so happy to find you! I can't wait to see his face on Christmas morning."

He lifted me out of the box and tucked me inside his coat, where it smelled like Yummy

Crumbs. He carried me outside in the cold. The stars twinkled in the dark sky. Cold white flakes drifted down from above. I lifted my muzzle and let them melt on the end of my nose.

"Puppy's first snow," Yummy Crumb Man said to me. Then he set me down on the ground. My breath steamed in the air, and the cold shot up my paws and sent shivers through me.

"Time to go potty, Ginger," Yummy Crumb Man said.

I didn't know what he wanted me to do. I had already piddled back in my box. In the cage, we piddled when and where we liked and it trickled out the bottom.

After I sniffed and explored a bit, he took me back inside. "Time to wrap you in ribbon!" Yummy Crumb Man said. He wrapped a crackly, shiny ribbon around my neck and tied it in a bow.

When he put me back in the box, I was happy to see that he had laid some rags on the bottom of it to cover the place where I had piddled and spilled water. I dug down into the rags, turned around three times, and went to sleep with my nose in my tail. I woke up in the middle of the night, piddled again, then went back to sleep.

The next thing I knew, someone was tearing through the top of the box. I was scared. I tried to dig myself a hole to hide in.

"Dylan—meet Ginger the Christmas Puppy!" Yummy Crumb Man said in a loud, happy voice.

"Remember the puppy you saw in the pet shop window?" Dylan's Mother said. "Now Ginger's all yours!"

"Dinger!" Dylan cried. He yanked me out of the box by the legs and hugged the breath out of me. I wanted to give him a little nip to tell him

he was being too rough, but he was squeezing me
so hard I could barely move.

"Be gentle, sweetheart," Dylan's Mother said.

Dylan dropped me on the floor and turned
away. I shook myself, and the next time I looked
up, there was paper flying through the air and
bright lights swirling and lots of tasty-smelling

food they took away just before I could get at it.
Dylan was tearing open other boxes and squealing
with excitement. I was excited, too. I thought there
might be more puppies in the other boxes. I kept
my eye out, but sadly, I was the only puppy. There
were other things, though: shiny things, things that
made noise, things that whirred and buzzed and

made me bark. There was a soft blue fuzzy thing with big, droopy ears that reminded me of Floppy Ears. I grabbed hold of one of his ears and pulled. Blue Floppy Ears didn't fight back, so I dragged him off into a corner to Play.

"Oh, no! Don't let Ginger chew your new stuffed bunny rabbit," Dylan's Mother said. "Remember, Dylan, puppies like to chew."

Yummy Crumb Man pulled at Blue Floppy Ears. I held on tight. This was fun!

"This isn't a game, Ginger," Yummy Crumb Man growled at me.

If it wasn't, I'd like to know *what* it was! In the end, I let him win because he ripped the thing right out of my mouth. I licked my chops and wagged my tail to show there were no hard feelings.

After that, I looked around for more Play. And then the urge to piddle came upon me. It was a sharp, shivery feeling that started at the back of my neck and ran down my spine to the base of my tail. I walked on stiff legs, looking for a good place to squat.

Then I realized all that bright, crackling paper would do nicely. I pawed at it, looking for the exact right spot.

"Shouldn't we take her out to go potty?" Dylan's Mother said in a worried voice. Mothers are such worriers.

"After I get this toy tool bench put together," Yummy Crumb Man said.

He was lying on the floor under a big tree with sweet-smelling branches. The Tree was calling out to me. *Come piddle here!* it said to me.

"Here I come!" I said to the Tree as I went over and squatted. *Ahhh!*

Just then, somebody screamed.

"Donald, I told you we should take her out! Do something! She's going under the Christmas tree!"

Yummy Crumb Man leapt to his feet and loomed over me. He glared. I froze. I ducked my head. My tail went between my legs.

"Bad dog!" he said. He took my head in his big hands and rubbed my nose in the piddle puddle. That wasn't right! The piddle that had frozen inside me came trickling down my leg.

"Oh, no, you don't!" he said. He picked me up by my scruff, carried me across the room, and set me down hard outside in the freezing cold.

"You can't just leave her out there," Dylan's Mother said.

"Sure I can. The yard's fenced in. She'll be fine," Yummy Crumb Man said. "She can stay out there until we're finished." He slid the door shut in my face.

Through the window, I saw the three of them gathered around my Tree. They were laughing and playing and having a good time. The yard was a cold, strange place. There was no one to play with. The world was too big. I wanted back inside, where there were people and it was warm. I got up on my hind legs and beat my fists against the window and whimpered, *Let me in! Let me in!* Then I sank to my haunches and made Sad Eyes at them.

"Awww," said Dylan's Mother, looking out at me. She looked even sadder than I did.

When Yummy Crumb Man let me back in, it was like the little boy remembered I was there. He played with me. He chased me and tried to grab my tail, but I was too fast for him. He reached out and got hold of the ribbon around my neck. I gagged. Then the ribbon came undone. I started chewing on the loose end. Dylan grabbed the other end. I

tugged. He tugged. This was good Play! Finally, I tugged so hard that Dylan let go and fell down on his backside. I won! Dylan opened his mouth and wailed.

"Mama!" he cried. "Dinger bad goggie!"

Dylan was a sore loser!

Dylan's Mother ran over. "What happened, Dylan? Did Ginger hurt you?"

Dylan kept crying until they gave him the little hammer from his tool bench. Then he started banging on everything in sight, and that cheered him up in no time. Meanwhile, I had the ribbon to myself, so I hunkered down and really started eating it. It turns out, ribbon is very salty, which is good, but very hard to swallow, which is bad. I started choking on the ribbon, but luckily I was able to cough it up. It made a hot, wet mess on the floor.

Yummy Crumb Man saw this and growled again. "What are you into *now*?"

I slinked off into a corner. Later, when no one was looking, I went back under the Tree and piddled. I have to admit, I really liked that Tree. I was sad when they finally took it down. After that, I always went back to the spot where the Tree had been to piddle. They put a nice fluffy rug in its place. It wasn't as nice as the Tree, but it served the purpose.

VET MAN

Imagine how unhappy I was to find myself back in another box on wheels! This one wasn't as big as the Truck. Dylan's Mother called it the Car. I sat in the Car on the seat next to Dylan's Mother. *Had I done something to make my pack unhappy? Had I chewed too many Shoes?* I was trying hard not to chew more than my share, but every time they found me with a Shoe they would make a big, noisy fuss. The noise was upsetting enough, but then there was the Newspaper. Yummy Crumb Man rolled up the Newspaper and bopped me on the head with it whenever I did something he didn't like. It didn't hurt so much, but it made me scared and nervous. And what do I do when I'm nervous? You guessed it. I either squat and piddle or look around for something to chew.

As if she sensed how worried I was, Dylan's Mother said to me, "It's okay, Ginger girl. Everything is going to be all right."

I didn't believe her for a minute because she sounded as nervous as I felt. Then she stopped the Car and clipped my leash to my collar. *What's going on?* They almost never took me for walks. I usually did my business in the backyard. I shook my head and wriggled my body to try to get rid of the leash.

Dylan's Mother came around to the other side of the Car and opened the door. She tugged the leash hard—so hard I stopped struggling. She said, "Jump down, Ginger. You're getting too big for me to carry now."

I tumbled down onto the ground and looked up at her, my tongue hanging out. *Was this what you wanted?*

"Good girl, Ginger!" Dylan's Mother said.

I wagged my tail. Maybe this wasn't going to be as bad as I thought. Maybe she was taking me somewhere to Play. I romped along beside her for a ways until we walked up some steps and she opened a door. Right away, my ears perked forward and my nose started twitching.

I smelled Puppy and Dog and other animals, too.

"Come, Ginger," Dylan's Mother said.

I followed her into a room where she sat down and said, "Stay." Where would I go with a leash on? I sat at her feet and looked around. There were other dogs sitting on the laps of their two-leggers or, like me, on the floor. Right next to me was a sleek, furry thing in a box. It had small ears and a long, slithery tail. It wasn't a dog.

Hi there! I said, wagging my tail.

The sleek, furry thing went bristly all over and spat at me.

"Be nice to the kitty cat, Ginger," Dylan's Mother told me, holding on tight to my leash.

Hey, I wasn't the one with the bad attitude! Cats! Who needed them?

There were dogs of all shapes and sizes. One of them rolled his eyes at me, as if he couldn't be bothered. Another strained against his leash and tried to be friendly. I wanted to be friendly, too, and to get a good, deep whiff of him. Maybe we could play! But Dylan's Mother had other plans.

She stood up. "Come on, Ginger. It's our turn," she said, pulling on my leash.

I didn't want to leave the friendly dog, but she dragged me by the leash into another room where I was the only dog. A woman who smelled like a dozen different dogs lifted me up and put me on a table. Who were all these strange dogs I smelled on her? What was going to happen to me?

"And how are we today, Ginger?" the woman asked. She seemed friendly and interested in knowing how I felt.

I'm a nervous wreck, since you asked, I said. Then I let out an anxious whine.

She stroked my back. "You'll be okay, Ginger. No one's going to hurt you." She set me on a cold, slippery plate and held me there while she fiddled with some dials.

"She's putting on weight nicely," Friendly

Woman said, running her hands over my coat and lifting my tail. "I'd say she's a little under three months old. Can I ask where you got her?"

"From the pet shop," Dylan's Mother said. "She was a Christmas gift for our two-year-old son, Dylan."

"If I were you, I wouldn't mention that detail to the doctor," Friendly Woman said. "He doesn't approve of puppies for Christmas. He says Christmas is exciting enough without bringing a new puppy into it. On Christmas morning, puppies tend to get lost in the shuffle."

"Oh," said Dylan's Mother.

Friendly Woman stuck something cold and slippery into my butt.

Yikes! I yipped. That wasn't very friendly!

She ran her hands over me. "Easy, girl," she whispered. "Just taking your temperature."

"And you haven't had any trouble?" Friendly Woman asked Dylan's Mother.

Dylan's Mother laughed. "Other than her peeing all over the house and chewing my shoes to shreds?"

"That's a puppy for you," said Friendly Woman. Whatever she had stuck inside of me, she pulled out. *That* was a relief! "She looks nice and healthy to me, although the vet will check her out more thoroughly. Some of the dogs that come from the pet shop have real issues."

"Really? Why is that?" Dylan's Mother asked.

"They come from puppy mills," Friendly Woman said.

"What are puppy mills?"

"Places that raise puppies for profit with no regard for the health and welfare of the puppies or their mothers," said Friendly Woman. "Some of the puppies that come in here have all sorts of problems. Diseases and genetic disorders and behavior issues far worse than Ginger's."

"That sounds terrible," Dylan's Mother said. I heard worry creep into her voice. "Do you think Ginger came from a puppy mill?"

"It's pretty likely, since most pet stores get their puppies from puppy mills," Friendly Woman said. "Next time you want a dog—if there is a next time—my advice is that you try adopting from a shelter."

"Thanks," said Dylan's Mother, "but we've got our hands full with Ginger at the moment. I had no idea how much work raising a puppy is. Almost as much as raising a child."

"Some people have no business raising puppies. It's a big commitment," Friendly Woman said, sounding not all that friendly. She carried me into another room and set me down on a table covered with paper. The paper was slippery and my paws scrabbled against it. I got worried all over again.

"The doctor will be with you in a minute," Friendly Woman said.

I felt Dylan's Mother's hands on me, quick and nervous.

A while later, a man came in.

"Don't be nervous, Ginger. This is the vet," Dylan's Mother whispered to me.

He didn't have a Newspaper with him, so I relaxed a little. Then he started feeling me all over with his hands. They were strong but gentle hands, and I began to calm down. He smelled like Fur and Soap. He poked and prodded me. He peered in my ears and looked in my mouth and nose and put something cold up against my belly.

"You're lucky. Her heart's sound. So are her

eyes and ears and skin and teeth. No ticks, no fleas,
sound joints, no tummy troubles that I can feel, no
umbilical hernia," Vet Man said. Then he bunched
up my skin and pricked me with something sharp
that made me twitch.

43

Ow—what was that? I yipped.

"It's okay, girl," Vet Man said as he stroked my fur. Then he said to Dylan's Mother, "I've just given her a five-way vaccination. Bring her back in a month and we'll give her another round. Then we'll talk about spaying her."

"Spaying?" said Dylan's Mother.

"Females should be spayed before their first heat, which is anywhere from five to eight months," Vet Man said. "That way, she won't whelp."

"Whelp?"

"Get pregnant and have puppies," Vet Man said.

"But wouldn't it be nice to let her have puppies?"

"Nice?" Vet Man said. "There are more than enough puppies in the world as it is, thanks to puppy mills and backyard breeders." He gave me

a scratch behind my ears in just the right place. "You're a good girl, aren't you?" he said to me.

You bet I am, I said. I grinned, and my hind leg *thump-thump-thump*ed against the paper on the table.

He laughed softly and ran his hands over my coat. "She's a beautiful golden retriever. Sometimes even puppy mills turn out a perfectly fine animal, if only by accident."

"Thank you, I think. Will she learn to go potty outdoors soon?" Dylan's Mother asked.

"Only if you train her," said Vet Man. "My vet tech will give you a pamphlet on your way out."

"And what about the chewing?"

"Puppies chew. Does she have any chew toys?"

"Only the ones she takes from my son," Dylan's Mother said with a nervous chuckle.

"Try giving her some of her own."

As I left that place I thought I wouldn't mind going back someday, even if it involved another sharp jab. But as it happened, I never saw Vet Man again. Because one day, when I was about four months old, Dylan slammed my tail with his toy hammer. He had tried this before, but in the past, I had moved my tail in time to avoid getting hit. This time, I was busy chewing off the head of a baby doll. And that hammer got me good. I was angry! It wasn't right, Dylan hitting me so hard. I decided it was time to teach him a lesson. So I nipped him. It was just the tiniest nip, enough to let him know not to try that again.

Dylan howled and flung the hammer at my head. I ducked, ran into the corner, and hid. Dylan's Mother came running. Dylan held out his hand and then pointed at me. "Bad goggie bit!"

"Ginger *bit you*?" Dylan's Mother said. "Let me

see." She swept him up in her arms and ran off with him.

I could hear them: Dylan sniffling and Dylan's Mother cooing. Dylan stopped crying almost right away, but Dylan's Mother was the one who was upset now. A few minutes later, they came back. She was still carrying Dylan. He was wearing a great big bandage on his finger. I hope you will believe me when I tell you that I hadn't even broken the skin. In my brief life with Dylan I knew one thing for sure, and that was the smaller the boo-boo, the bigger the bandage.

When Yummy Crumb Man came home that night, he peeled off the bandage and looked at Dylan's hand. "We're lucky it wasn't a whole lot worse," he said.

He loomed over me and glared. Before I could even tuck my tail between my legs, he grabbed me

by the collar and dragged me down into the base-
ment where it smelled Cold and Damp. Upstairs,
I could hear them stomping around and yelling
and crying.

"I'm sorry," said Yummy Crumb Man, "but we
can't take any chances. Dylan's a child. You saw on
the news the other night where the boy got mauled
by his father's dog."

"That was some other breed!" Dylan's Mother said. "Goldens are supposed to be great with children."

"Maybe Dylan's just not ready for a pet," Yummy Crumb Man said.

Dylan was crying and begging them to let him keep me.

"It's for the best, honey," said Dylan's Mother.

"Daddy and Mommy made a mistake," said Yummy Crumb Man. "We'll get another dog . . . when you're older and more responsible."

If you ask me, Dylan wasn't the irresponsible one, but nobody asked me. Nobody ever asked me.

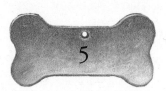

GIVE ME SHELTER

When Yummy Crumb Man dropped me off at the shelter, I was a little sad. I was going to miss licking Dylan's face. There was always lots of yummy stuff like jelly smeared around his jowls. But that pack made me nervous. I never knew what they were going to do. I don't think they knew, either. And I would not miss getting my tail hammered, or being bopped on the head with a Newspaper, or having my nose rubbed in piddle and poop. All things considered, I was ready to make a fresh start.

Another vet, this one a female, looked me over and checked me for fleas and worms. After Lady Vet had given me the vaccination my former pack was supposed to have gotten for me but never did, I was put in a cage next to two other dogs, one white, and one white with brown spots.

Oh, joy! I thought. Besides that one visit with Vet Man, I hadn't been in such close contact with other dogs since I'd left my littermates at the pet shop. This was going to be fun! I bounded over to the wire. I wasn't going to let a little thing like a cage get in the way of Play. My eyes were wide, my ears were perked forward, my tail was straight out behind me. I stuck my nose through the wire. I just wanted to give them a sniff! Then the white dog bore down on me. Her forehead wrinkled, her lips peeled back from her teeth, and she growled,

This is my turf, little lady, and what I say goes.

Well, you didn't have to tell *me* twice! My ears went back, my tail drooped, and I licked the air between us. *Sure thing, Whitey,* I said. I was sweating through the pads of my feet, I was so nervous. I swiped the air with one paw to show her I really meant it. *You're the boss,* I told her.

When Alice comes through that door, I'm first in line for whatever she's got. You, Blondie, are last.

No problem, I said, and I skulked off into the corner, as far away from Whitey as I could get.

Then the one with spots came over to the wire, tail up, ears perked. She bowed before me, her paws splayed. *Don't mind my sister. She's a grump. Let's play!*

I was cautious at first. On stiff legs, tail high, I sniffed her through the wire. I turned around so she could sniff beneath my tail, and then I sniffed beneath hers. After that, she ducked back down again and got all goofy, tongue lolling on the floor. She pounced and started chasing me along the side of the cage. We ran back and forth and never once showed our teeth. It was fun!

Later, we lay around on either side of the cage wall, licking ourselves and scratching. *Tell me about this place,* I said to Spotty.

This is the place where New Owners come to find dogs, she said. *They take us out and look us over and play with us, and if they like what they see, they take us home with them. My sister and I just got here. Our owners were moving to an apartment where they couldn't have dogs. We'll probably have to go to different homes, but that's okay. My sister's a little bossy, as you can see. I could use a break from her.*

What happens if it doesn't work out at our new homes? I asked.

They return us, she said. *But it's not good to get returned. And it's not good when no one picks you at all.*

Why not? I asked.

Because then they put you down for the Never-Ending Nap.

I liked to nap as much as the next dog, but I had a bad feeling about this nap, so I changed the subject. *Who's Alice?*

She's the animal-control officer we all like the best, said Spotty.

Is she nice? I asked.

Nice? She's better than nice, said Spotty. *She's fair. She's tough with the tough dogs and gentle with the gentle ones. They say she has a weak spot for golden retrievers, so you're in luck, Blondie.*

As it turned out, Alice *was* nice. I guess you could say that I'm a friendly dog, so Alice was friendly with me when she came into my cage.

"I have a funny feeling," she said, "that you're not really a biter. You probably had a very good reason for biting that little boy . . . *not* that you did the right thing. You just couldn't help yourself. I'll tell you what: I'm going to give you the benefit of the doubt, Ginger old girl."

I liked that she called me by my name. She also knew where my Sweet Spot was, and she scratched me there until I grinned and my leg went *thump-thump-thump*. She brushed me and told me I had a beautiful coat. I could tell she had my best interests at heart. When a pack came in with a child just a little bigger than Dylan, looking for a golden retriever, Alice told them to look somewhere else.

"But she's such a beautiful animal!" the mother said as she stared longingly through the cage at me. I stared right back, wagging my tail to show that I was as well behaved as I was beautiful.

"She's got issues. Believe me when I say that she's not right for you," Alice said, without going into any of the unpleasantness about the hammer and the tail and the warning nip. Not to mention the puppy mill and the pet shop. Life is tough enough without having to drag around a lot of unpleasant history.

When the pack left the shelter, I looked after them with Sad Eyes.

"Cheer up, Ginger!" Alice said to me. "The right family for you is out there someplace, and we're going to find it."

But what was the right family for me?

The next day a tall, skinny man came in looking for a dog to run with him.

"I might have a dog for you," Alice said. "She's a golden retriever. They love to run. I don't think her last family took her out to run enough."

I'd never gotten much of a chance to run before, but I had a feeling I was going to like it. Skinny Man seemed gentle and soft-spoken. And he wasn't carrying a Newspaper. I went right up to him and wagged my tail and sniffed his fingers. He smelled like Wind and Rubber and Sweat. He even brought a toy with him, a Bouncy Ball. He bounced it. I followed it with my eyes. He caught it in his hands. Then he threw it. I ran to get it and

brought it back to him and let him take it from my mouth without any argument. He threw the ball again. I ran to get it and delivered it back into his hands. Skinny Man knew all about Play!

Alice made sure the man made a lot of promises about getting me spayed (*that* again!) and fencing in his yard and keeping me on a leash and taking me for nice long walks and feeding me good food. Then he put a brand-new collar around my neck with a jingly tag on it and hitched me to a leash. With hopes as high as my tail, I was all set to go to my new home.

Skinny Man took me outside to his funny-looking Car.

"This is my jeep, Ginger," Skinny Man said to me, opening the door. He slapped the seat. "Jump," he said.

I jumped into the jeep, and he gave me something tasty to eat. I wagged my tail. *Can we do that again?* I asked him. But he had already shut the door. He went to the other side of the jeep and climbed in next to me.

"We're going to have a lot of fun together, Ginger," he said.

I couldn't have agreed more.

"But let's get one thing straight at the outset," Skinny Man said. "We don't peep in the jeep."

My tail thumped against the back of the seat. I had no idea what he meant. *Sure thing, Skinny Man! Whatever you say.*

Then the jeep rolled forward. I started to get worried, but he shot a hand out and patted me until I calmed down. The jeep window was open just wide enough to poke my nose out. Mysterious scents came streaming in all at once.

Ahhh! The wind ruffled my ears, and my nose

twitched. *The smell of it!* It was enough to make a dog dizzy. What a world! This really was a fresh start.

The days that followed lived up to my expectations. Every morning, Skinny Man took me out for a long, brisk walk. I sniffed at the places where other dogs had piddled, and I squatted in those places and added my piddle to the general discussion. When I did this, Skinny Man praised me and said, "Good girl, Ginger." And I felt good. I liked being good for him, and I liked being outside.

Skinny Man had rules, and he made them all very clear to me. I was not allowed to jump up on any of the chairs or couches, except for the one he had covered with a sheet. That couch was mine, and when he had guests, they always asked me if it was all right to share my couch. I was happy to have the company. I was not allowed in his bed, but I could sleep on the floor next to his bed. When I broke the rules, all he had to do was glare at me and say, *"Ginger!"* in a stern voice and I fell instantly (or, well, *almost* instantly) into line. In the two seasons I lived with him, I always knew where I stood.

Skinny Man went out into the world without me almost every day. I spent the mornings by the front window, waiting for him to come home. Halfway through the day, he would come up the walk. I'd leap to my feet and race to the door, wagging my tail. When he opened the door, I jumped up on him and hugged him. He stroked my head and ears and let me lick his face. He took me out for a walk before he did anything else, and I appreciated his thoughtfulness. (A dog can only hold it for so long.) The times I made mistakes, he never rubbed my nose in it. He acted like he understood. After the walk, when we came back inside, he would sit down and eat. I would plunk down at his feet and watch him.

"Don't beg, Ginger," he'd say.

Who was begging? I was just watching the food move around in his mouth and occasionally licking my lips and moaning faintly. Sometimes little bits dropped on the floor and he didn't mind if I licked them up. It's not like I didn't have my own food, which he fed me twice a day.

After he had eaten and cleaned up, he went away again, and I spent the afternoons sleeping and chewing on my Rubber Bone or my Bouncy Ball.

The evenings were the best time of day because that was when he took me out to run with him. He was a good runner for a two-legger. We ran through the park, which smelled like Squirrel and Rabbit and Damp Leaves. Now and then we met up with other dogs on leashes. Skinny Man would slow down and stop running and give us dogs a chance to meet and greet.

"Beautiful dog," said one of the Other Owners. I felt her eyes on me. I looked away quickly. I knew when to play shy. "Is she a purebred?"

"I don't know," said Skinny Man. "I adopted her from the shelter."

"Even so . . . she's got nice lines," said Other Owner as she patted me. She seemed to be waiting for him to say something nice about her own poufy-headed dog, who was poking his pointy nose beneath my tail.

"Is your, err . . . poodle a purebred?" Skinny Man asked.

Poufy-Head lifted his nose from beneath my tail and snorted. *As if he has to ask! They don't get much purer than me.*

"He'd better be," Other Owner said. "I got him from a top breeder and paid a small fortune."

Money is no object when it comes to canine perfection, Poufy-Head said.

Poufy-Head certainly had a high opinion of himself, I'll say that.

Life continued in this fashion: walking, running, meeting, greeting, chewing Bouncy Ball and Rubber Bone while I waited for Skinny Man to come home. One day, Skinny Man took me to New Vet and I got really sleepy, and when I woke up, I had a whopping huge bellyache. Skinny Man was very gentle with me that night. He gave me a little food and water, and afterward, I licked the place on my belly where all the fur had been shaved away. For a few days, my belly itched something fierce. Sometimes I'd drag myself across the rug just to relieve the itching. But after a few days, I forgot about it and got on with my life. *So that was spaying? Big deal.*

The Really Bad Thing didn't happen until sometime after the spaying. I was lying at Skinny Man's feet while he sat in his chair with a Newspaper. He always kept the Newspaper to himself, so it didn't bother me much anymore. Just then, that little thing he carried around in his pocket jingled. He took out the Jingly Thing and spoke to it.

"Oh, no! Is she all right?" he asked, sitting up and dropping the Newspaper on my head. He sounded very upset and nervous. I got up, shook off the Newspaper, and stared up at him. *What? What? What?* I wanted to know. If he was worried, I was worried, too.

He got up and began walking back and forth, still talking on the Jingly Thing. I stayed right at his feet, trotting from the front door to the kitchen counter and back again. When he stopped, I stopped. He kept running his hands through his hair. Then he said, "I'll get the next flight out. I just need to find somebody to take care of Ginger. A dog walker."

I heard my name and wagged my tail. But what

was this Dog Walker business? I was a little worried. Had I done something to displease him? I thought I had been doing almost everything right. I sank down onto my haunches and began to whimper. He got down on the floor with me and took me in his arms. He rocked me and sobbed into my neck. "My mom's sick, Ginger. Real sick. She might not make it. I have to go and be with her."

I wagged my tail and licked his salty, wet face. I was willing to do whatever it took to make him feel better.

"I wish I could take you with me, but I can't. My dad's allergic to dogs. I'll have to find a dog walker for you while I'm gone."

There it was again. *Dog Walker.* I figured, considering how upset he was, that it couldn't be good.

6

THE WILD BUNCH

Skinny Man went away that same night after running around the house and gathering up a bunch of his clothes and other stuff. He left me a bowl of water and a bowl of food. I was alone all night. I had rarely been alone all night, and I didn't like it.

The next morning, Dog Walker showed up. She was nice enough. She patted me and filled my empty bowls. But the walk she took me on wasn't very long. She was in a hurry to get back to the house and practically dragged me there. I went along with her, though. After all, maybe Skinny Man was coming home, and I wanted to be there when he did. Still, a dog had to do her business, didn't she? Dog Walker tapped her foot while I pooped. As she scooped my poop into a plastic bag, she made a face and said, "Yuck!"

Yuck yourself, I wanted to say. *And I suppose your poop smells like roses?*

That day, I waited a long time for Skinny Man to come home. When Dog Walker came instead, my tail drooped, but I went out with her and did my business as quickly as I could. When I went back into the house, I didn't go to the couch that was covered with a sheet. I jumped up onto Skinny Man's chair and curled up nose to tail. He would never let me do this if he were home. I hoped he would come home and tell me, "Ginger, get down!

You know that's not your chair." I would have given anything to hear him say that. I stayed there all night, hoping he would come.

Every time I heard a car go by, I would leap up and run to the window. But Skinny Man never came. I was very sad. *Where was Skinny Man? Was Skinny Man going to go away and never come back the way Mother had?* It made me very nervous, and when I'm nervous, remember what I do? That's right. I piddle and I look around for something to chew.

When Dog Walker came back the next morning and saw the puddle of piddle by the door, I could tell she was very upset. She got down on her hands and knees and scrubbed it. I went up and sniffed the puddle. Did she need any help? She pushed me away. Then she found the magazines I had shredded and the Shoe I had chewed and she said in a loud voice, "Bad, *bad* Ginger!"

I heaved a sigh. She had some nerve calling me bad. She was bad, if you ask me—a bad, *bad* Dog Walker!

Bad Dog Walker quickly shoved the magazines and the Shoe in the kitchen garbage and took me out for the shortest walk I have ever taken. And guess what? She didn't even scoop up my poop! She left it there for someone to step in. Then she hustled me back to the house and shut the door and walked away. As soon as Bad Dog Walker was gone, I dug in the garbage and retrieved the shredded magazines and the Shoe. They don't call me a retriever for nothing.

The next day, Bad Dog Walker came back and didn't even say good morning to me. She filled a great big bowl with food and a great big bowl with water—more food and drink than I had ever gotten at one time. She said to me, "I'll be back to-morrow afternoon. This ought to hold you. You'll be fine." She spread out some newspaper by the door where I had piddled before. "Go potty there if you can't hold it," she said.

I had no idea what she was talking about. I had already found a better place to piddle. It was in Skinny Man's closet, where his Shoes were. I wanted to make sure he would find me when he came home . . . *if* he came home. I was beginning to lose hope.

"Is it me, or does it stink in here?" she asked. Then she went over to the window and raised it higher than Skinny Man ever had. I think he wanted to protect me from Dangerous Things Outside, but Bad Dog Walker obviously didn't care. The window was wide open now, and through it wafted all sorts of scents. I lifted my nose and breathed them in deeply. They didn't smell at all dangerous. In fact, they smelled wonderful—and they seemed to be calling to me. *Ginger! Come out and sniff us. Come walk on the wild side.*

After Bad Dog Walker left, I gobbled down all the food and lapped up all the water. I was so full, you'd think I wouldn't be able to do what I did next. But I did. I took a good running start and leapt right through that window screen and out

into the front yard. I shook myself off and looked around. There I was, as free as the chattering birds that flew from branch to branch. Scold away, birdies. What did I care? *I was free!*

Do you know what I did then? I took *myself* for a walk. I took myself to all the places Skinny Man took me. There was no one to scoop up my poop, so I kicked it aside and went on my merry way. I was headed for the park. I didn't need Skinny Man to run. I could run by myself. I must have looked mighty bold. But deep down, do you know what I was thinking? I was thinking that maybe Skinny Man was somewhere in the park. Maybe he had gone to the park without me and gotten lost. Maybe I could find him and bring him home and everything would be just the way it used to be.

Up ahead, I saw Other Owner with Poufy-Head. She called out to me in a scolding tone,

"Ginger! What are you doing out here without your father?"

I went up to Poufy-Head and danced in front of him, all excited. *Look at me, I'm free! Don't you wish you were, too?*

Freedom is for lowlifes, he said. *You're going to be sorry you ever tasted freedom.*

Other Owner lunged for me, but I was too fast for her. I danced away from her, and then I ran until I couldn't hear her calling my name anymore. On and on I ran, deeper and deeper into the park. I chased a squirrel. I sniffed and scratched at a rabbit hole. I rolled in a nice dead bird. Now I smelled just like the park, like something wild. Oh, it felt so good! Poufy-Head was wrong! Being free was the way to be.

Then it got dark, and bit by bit, it didn't feel so good to be free. The shadows scared me. Nothing smelled familiar. The world was filled with Dangerous Things. Skinny Man had never taken me this deep into the park. There were deer, and raccoons, and a skunk that I backed away from so fast I almost fell into a stream. I leaned down and lapped up some water. Freedom made me thirsty. Hungry, too. I found some garbage and ate it all up. It tasted a little ripe, but I wasn't choosy. Then I found a box of slimy stuff. I knew what it was right away. Skinny Man liked to eat it sometimes. A man in a Car delivered it to the door. It was Pizza Pie. I had just started chowing down on the oily mess when I heard a deep snort.

Put down the pizza, someone said.

I dropped the Pizza Pie and found myself face to face with the ugliest, meanest-looking dog that I had ever laid eyes on. Though his ribs poked through his mangy coat, he was all muscle. He had one beady black eye, and the other was all shriveled up in its socket. He had a tattered ear and a snaggletooth and one leg that was twisted and shorter than the other three.

Step away from the box, he said.

I did as I was told. Suddenly, two other dogs shouldered their way out of the bushes: a tiny little yappy thing and a shaggy hound. They nosed up behind Snaggletooth. Yappy and Shaggy ate what Snaggletooth didn't want. I was too scared to do anything but stare. None of them paid me any mind.

After they had eaten, Snaggletooth came over to me. *You still here?* he said. I stood there stiffly while he sniffed me. I was careful not to look him in the eyes—or should I say *eye*? I did *not* want to tangle with him.

You're pretty cute, said Snaggletooth when he

was finished inspecting me. *Big, too. I think you could be useful. Want to join our gang?*

I didn't have anything better to do. And maybe they could help me track down Skinny Man. *Sure,* I said.

And that was the beginning of my days living as an outlaw. We had a cozy-enough den inside a thicket of bushes where Snag and his gang had dug

out a nice deep sleeping pit. The summer months were good to us. There were plenty of picnickers in the park, and the garbage cans were overflowing with good stuff to eat. We'd wait until dark and then raid the cans, me and Snag and Shaggy and Yappy. When we couldn't tip them over, as the tallest one, I'd leap up and dig around and spill things on the ground. Then we'd sift through it for the choicest bits: crusts of bread and rinds of melon and now and then a bone or some gristle. We ate it all, even if it made us sick, because we never knew when our next meal would come.

I'll never forget the night I raided this really ripe and overflowing can of garbage. I was standing up on my hind legs, digging around with my nose for the good, wet, stinky stuff, when something slashed me across the muzzle.

Yeeeouchie! I yelped, pulling back.

Rearing up on her hind legs, the raccoon in the trash barrel readied her fist to take another swipe at me.

I was here first, she hissed. *Beat it!*

I dropped down and ran around in circles, pawing my bloody muzzle. What did she have to go and do that for?

Then I hunkered down and licked my paw,

passing it over and over the bloody boo-boo.

Snaggletooth limped over to me and growled. *What are you doing sitting there with your paw on your nose? Go back in there and show her who owns these cans.*

Show her yourself, I said to Snaggletooth. But I could tell that Snag wasn't any more eager to take on a needle-fisted raccoon than I was. That night, we all went without dinner.

I was good and sick after the incident with the raccoon. My nose got all dry and warm. My muzzle was so tender I could barely open my mouth. It was starting to get frosty in the mornings outside our den. Some days, I just lay in the den while the others went out hunting for food. I slept and dreamt of running with Skinny Man and chasing my Bouncy Ball. Then one morning, I woke up and I felt much better. But I sure was hungry! I don't think my stomach had ever been so empty.

I went back to raiding the cans, but there were slim pickings now. Because it was colder, fewer two-leggers came to the park to eat. It seemed like we were always hungry. Have you ever been hungry? I mean *really* hungry? It's a terrible, gnawing feeling—a dull, churning ache in your guts that, day and night, sleeping or waking, never goes away. *Maybe,* I began to think, *Poufy-Head was right, after all. Maybe freedom isn't all it's cracked up to be.*

For a few days, it turned warm again and the two-leggers poured back into the park. We came upon some small ones playing in the open field near the stream. The rest of the gang hightailed it for the woods. Two-leggers scared them, but they didn't scare me. They were laughing and talking and tossing a flat spinning thing back and forth to each other. I couldn't resist. I ran after the Spinny

Thing and caught it on my first try.

"Wow! Good catch!" a little one said.

Then her mother came running over. "Leave the dog alone, kids. It's wild. It might have rabies. Let it have the Frisbee. I'll buy you another one."

The little ones backed away and left me the Spinny Thing. But it wasn't much fun without anyone to throw it. So I left it there and ran off to find the gang. What had just happened? Two-leggers had always liked me. Had I become a lowlife? Had some of Snaggletooth's wildness rubbed off on me? His fleas certainly had, I knew that much. It was almost enough to make me wish for Flea Bath— but not quite!

This was about the time I started chasing the Truck. This particular Truck picked up the garbage cans and swallowed the garbage in its giant maw. It made a terrible grinding noise that hurt my ears. Whenever the Truck came, I ran after it and barked. It needed to know that this was *our* turf and *our* garbage. One time the Truck stopped and a man got out and chased me with a stick. The stick cracked me on the back and I walked crooked for days.

Serves you right for chasing Trucks, Snag said to me. *You'd better stop doing that. You'll bring the Dog-catchers down on us if you're not careful.*

What are Dogcatchers? I asked.

They come with buzzing sticks and nets and they catch us and carry us off to the Big Dog House, Snag said. *They say it's for our own good, but our kind never last long there. Sooner or later, it's the Never-Ending Nap for us.*

What did he mean by *our kind*? I wondered. *What had I gotten myself into?*

I vowed to stop chasing Trucks, but as it turned

out, the Dogcatchers were already onto us. They came the next day. Snag and Shaggy and Yappy got one whiff and skedaddled, leaving me to face them alone. They didn't look dangerous to me, and besides, there was something familiar about one of them.

"Ginger? Is that you?" a voice called out.

I looked up and wagged my tail a little, just to show that I might be Ginger, depending on who was asking.

"That *is* you," said the voice. "Ginger, what have you been up to?"

I wagged my tail a little more. The two-legger came up to me and I sniffed her hand. Then my tail got going. I knew who this was! This was my old friend Alice, the animal-control lady.

Bruce's Farm

"It turns out, *Ginger* is the feral dog who's been giving those sanitation trucks a run for their money!" Alice said to Lady Vet, who was giving me a thorough going-over. Then Alice said to me, "Do you have any idea how many complaints we've had about you and your gang?"

My tail froze. Was she angry with me or happy to see me again? I think she was both. It was very confusing.

I had already suffered through Flea Bath, and now I was sitting on the same slippery paper-covered table where I had sat before. This time, Lady Vet was not so happy to see me. She kept shaking her head and running her hand over my coat. "I barely recognize her," she said. "This can't be the same beautiful dog who was in here last spring."

What was she talking about? Of course I was the same dog. I was me: Ginger the golden retriever, Puppy Number One of Six, pride of Batch Three, Cage Nine, big as life and twice as beautiful.

"She's not exactly a good candidate for adoption," Lady Vet said.

"No, she isn't. At least, not the way she's looking right now. I tried to contact her former owner, but he's moved away with no forwarding address," Alice said. "I have a friend over near Lakeville. He rescues and rehabilitates dogs and cats—the worst cases. I'm going to give him a call and see if he has room for our girl here."

I rode with Alice in her dog-smelling Car. It was too cold for open windows to poke my nose out of, but I enjoyed the warmth of her Car and I liked being with her. She talked to me all the while.

"You'll like my friend Bruce," she said. "He's my hero. He takes in animals that no one else wants—the biters and the misfits, the old and the infirm, as well as juvenile delinquents like you. He feeds them and deworms them and loves them and tries to find good homes for them. But he's very fussy about who takes his animals. He'd rather keep an animal for the rest of its life than give it to the wrong home. And you, Ginger, have had your share of wrong homes. Maybe next time, you'll be lucky."

I didn't know what she was talking about, but I felt hopeful. When we got there, I liked the way Bruce smelled. He smelled like Dog and Cat and Old Boots. No sooner had we arrived than those big white flakes came falling down from the sky. A dog bounded along behind him. I stopped and let her smell me. That was when I noticed she only had three legs.

"Looks like Tripod approves of Ginger," Bruce said to Alice.

Hey, I said to the dog. *Where did your other leg go?*

I ran after a car and got tangled up in the wheel. It broke my leg. The break healed badly and they had to cut the leg clean off. That's when Bruce took me because my owners didn't want the trouble of a three-legged dog. Although I'm no trouble, as you can see.

You get around pretty good, I told her, after she

had let me sniff under her tail a bit.

You bet I do. I belong to the boss, so that makes me the boss. Eat your food and stay out of trouble and maybe a human pack will come along and be your furever *family. If not, don't worry. Bruce will keep you. That's the thing about Bruce. He would rather keep you than see you go to a bad home.*

The more I hear about Bruce, I said, *the more I like him.*

Alice said goodbye and kissed me on the muzzle, right where the raccoon had left her mark. She scratched me in my Sweet Spot until I grinned and thumped my leg.

"Your reflexes are still in fine working order," she said. "And pretty soon the rest of you will be tip-top, too."

She left me with Bruce. He and Tripod took me into a big, old barn that was full of pens with

dogs in them. They all barked and wanted to know what I was doing there. I was a little shy, but Tripod liked me well enough, so I figured I was in.

We walked past a big cage that was full of cats.

It was the biggest cage I had ever seen. It had all sorts of things for them to climb on and hide in. It looked like fun, but one of the cats raised her back to me and told me to mind my own business. That's a cat for you. Standoffish.

"This is where you'll be staying, Ginger," Bruce said to me. It was a small pen. There was another dog inside. She was old and slow and stinky, but she didn't seem to mind having a roommate.

"This is Elka," said Bruce. "She's a golden retriever like you, but she's a senior citizen. Like a lot of goldens who have been overbred, she has hip dysplasia, so she doesn't get around too well these days."

I went to Elka and wagged my tail.

Easy does it, whippersnapper, she said to me. *I'm not as spry as I used to be.*

I sat down at a respectful distance. *That's okay.*

I can play by myself. I didn't want to tell her that she smelled like a dead possum, so I just said, *Thanks for having me here.*

Bruce put down separate food and water dishes for me. "Don't worry, Ginger. Elka doesn't have much of an appetite these days, so she won't be trying to eat your food. We're going to fatten you up in no time."

Then he went over and pushed at the wall. There was a little rubber door there, just big enough for me to squeeze through. "Out there, you can have yourself a nice fresh-air run anytime you like. You can do your business out there, too."

I poked my nose out the rubber door. Sure enough, there was a small fenced-in yard. There were even some toys lying around. I went back to my bowl. Bruce was gone, but he had left me plenty of food that I quickly ate up. I had learned to eat quickly from my days in the wild. This wasn't the wild, but I was still a little nervous.

You can Play with my toys if you like, Elka told me. *I'm too old and tired to Play these days.*

She was right about that. I sleep a lot, but Elka slept almost all the time. She woke up to poke her nose around in her bowl or to go outside to poop—which I stayed clear of. It didn't look good and hard like mine. It looked more like soup.

Are you sick or something? I asked.

Not really. I'm just old, she said. *That's why my human pack didn't want me anymore. I can't control my bowels. But Bruce took me so I could have a little more time in the world. That's Bruce for you.*

That's what I wanted. Lots of time in the world to do the things I loved: Play and run and scratch and nap and poop and piddle. So I did what Bruce told me to do. I ate and I ran around in the yard and I took my worm medicine like a good dog. The snow melted and turned to mud. By that time, I was fat and my coat was shiny and those icky worms were flushed out of me.

One day when the air smelled green and sweet and muddy, a human pack came into the barn with Bruce. The boy passed close enough to my pen for me to get a good whiff of him. He wasn't a tiny boy like Dylan. He was bigger, and I liked what I smelled. I wagged my tail, but he and the others walked right past my pen to the cat cage. There, the four of them stood and stared at the cats as if they were the most fascinating creatures in the world. I've noticed that cats have that effect on some people.

Hey! I said with a loud yip. *What about me?* I was fascinating, too! I was even better than fascinating. I knew about Play! I ran out to my yard, got my Bouncy Ball, and ran back to the edge of the pen. Can cats do that? Can cats play catch with a Bouncy Ball? Of course they can't! Give a cat a Bouncy Ball and she'll keep it for herself. I'd show that boy I was much more fun than a cat.

Bruce spoke to the human pack. "The cats in the other cage are pretty much feral, but these cats are their kittens. They've all been altered and are good to go."

"Do you see any ones you like?" the mother said to the boy in a soft voice.

The boy sounded sad. He scuffed the floor with his foot. "I want Peaches."

"I know you do, honey. I miss her, too, but Peaches isn't coming back. Peaches was his old cat," the mother explained to Bruce. "She had stomach cancer and we had to put her down a few weeks ago. Before she died, she adopted a stray kitten. The kitten has been lonely and we thought we'd adopt another cat to keep her company."

"That sounds like a good idea," said Bruce. "Take your pick."

Don't do it! I barked. The little boy turned his head and looked at me, almost as if he understood what I was saying. I tossed the ball up in the air and caught it neat as you please, just to show him what I could do. The boy's father was watching, too.

"That's a golden retriever, isn't it?" he said.

"She sure is," said Bruce. "Her name is Ginger. She was rescued from a park where she was running wild."

"She doesn't look wild to me," said the man. "In fact, she has great lines. I know. My mother raised goldens. I grew up with them. I keep telling my wife we should get a golden, but Corey's afraid of dogs."

"Is that true, Corey?" Bruce said in a gentle voice. "Are you afraid of dogs?"

Corey shook his head firmly. "I just like cats better." He was looking at me when he said this, so I could tell he might be just a little bit interested in dogs now.

Corey's Father said, "When he was a toddler, a big dog jumped up and knocked him down. He's nine now, but I think he might still be a little afraid."

"No, I'm not," Corey said. He didn't seem fearful. He seemed thoughtful. I sat on my haunches to make myself look smaller and ducked my head. I whimpered a little and rolled the ball ever so gently toward him.

"Hey, Corey, I think Ginger wants to play with you," said Corey's Father.

"If you want," said Bruce, "I can take her out into the yard and you can meet her."

The boy didn't say anything. I lay down and put my nose on my paws and peered up at him, making Sad Eyes. *Are you* sure *you don't want to play with me?* I whimpered softly. This boy, I tell you! He was just the right size for me. He would never take a hammer to me or pull my tail or squeeze the breath out of me or go away and never come back. This was a good boy. I knew it in my gut.

"Okay," said the boy in a small voice.

Yes! I bounded to my feet.

When Bruce took me out of the pen, I remembered to take the Bouncy Ball with me. We all went outside. While they walked, I romped around a little. As happy as I am, I am always a little happier the moment I step outside. I dropped the ball on the ground in front of the boy.

The boy hesitated. Then he picked up the ball quickly like he was afraid I'd get it first. He threw it. The ball sailed high into the air. I ran to the end of my leash but the ball was too far away for me to reach. I watched it *bounce-bounce-bounce* and I wagged my tail and barked. *No fair!* If I were free I would be all over that ball.

Corey's Father laughed. "Corey was in the Little League where we lived before. He's got quite an arm." Corey's Father went to get the ball. "Don't throw it quite so far, son. Make it a baby throw so she can reach it."

Corey tossed the Bouncy Ball into the air high above my head. I tracked it with my eyes and leapt up to catch it as it fell to the ground. Then I brought the ball over to Corey and dropped it at his feet. I

put my muzzle on my forelegs and looked up at him, tail wagging, waiting for more Play.

"This dog can play some serious ball!" Corey grinned. When he tossed the ball up in the air again, I caught it again. This time, I tried something different. I held the ball very lightly in my mouth and brought it to Corey. He snatched the ball out of my mouth.

"She let me take it!"

"She seems very eager to please," said Corey's Mother. *She got that right.*

"Retrievers have soft mouths," Corey's Father said. "That's how they're bred, to retrieve birds and other small game for hunters. Something tells me this dog hasn't always been wild. For one thing, she knows how to play ball."

"And she certainly seems to like you, Corey," Corey's Mother said.

"All I know," said Bruce, "is that this dog was a worm-ridden sack of skin and bones when she first came to me. She's had a rough time of it and she deserves better."

Corey went over to his father. His father leaned down while Corey whispered in his ear. Then Corey went to his mother and whispered to her. Smiling and looking at Corey's Father, she said, "It's okay with me if it's okay with you, dear."

"More than okay with me," Corey's Father said. He walked over to speak to Bruce.

Bruce listened, then sighed and shook his head. "I don't know. You guys came here to get a cat. . . . The boy and Ginger seem to get along well, but I have to know that she'll be safe in your home. Is the yard fenced in?"

"On the roadside, yes," said Corey's Father. "But the backyard faces on a lake."

Bruce shot me a happy look and said in a voice full of excitement, "Did you hear that, Ginger? These folks are offering you waterfront real estate."

"Retrievers *do* love water," said Corey's Father.

"Why don't you folks come to my office with me?" Bruce said. "I need to ask you some routine questions and there's some paperwork I need you to fill out."

As I went back to my pen, I tried not to get my hopes up.

I don't know if they liked me enough to be my furever family . . . , I said to Elka.

Elka's head popped up from her paws. *Are you kidding me? I was watching from the yard. They were crazy about you. You have a one-way ticket out of here. And if for some reason it doesn't work out, Bruce will let you come back. But listen, kid. If you do come back—and I hope you don't—you probably won't find me here.*

Why? Are you getting a new home, too? I asked.

Who, me? said Elka. *No, this is my last home. Pretty soon, I'll be crossing the Rainbow Bridge.*

I've heard about that bridge, I said. *Where is it, anyway?*

No one knows where it is, but it leads to the place where all dogs go sooner or later, Elka said. *It's the place where the bones are big and juicy and the car wheels can't hurt you and the squirrels are slow enough that you can always catch them.*

Oh, I said. It sounded nice, but I would much rather go to a good home. We wished each other good luck and good sniffing, and then Elka dropped her head back onto her paws and went to sleep. She was still sleeping when the boy came to get me.

FUREVER

When I first went home, I cased the house and sniffed everything in sight while my new human pack stood around and watched me closely. I could tell they were anxious and afraid I wouldn't like the place. But I liked it fine. The thing was, it smelled like Cat. I smelled Cat everywhere but there was no Cat. This was a mystery to me.

One door was shut. I sniffed the space at the bottom of the door and the scent of Cat poured into my nostrils. *Oh, yeah.* There was no doubt about it. There was a cat in this house, and it was in that locked room. I scratched on the door. I wanted at that cat.

"Buttercup's in there," Corey said. "She's little, so my mom doesn't want you to meet her yet. She wants you two to get off to a good start."

I wagged my tail and dipped my head. *Okay.* New house, new rules. Later, for the cat. I got it.

I had plenty to keep me occupied without concerning myself with Buttercup. The backyard was big and fenced in, except for a wide part that faced the lake, where a long wooden dock jutted out into the water. I wasn't sure about the water. It moved and lapped and sloshed and went on forever. It seemed to be calling to me. *Come on in!*

I can see you fine from here, I told the lake. I barked at the waves and got down on my front legs, but the waves didn't want to play.

There were ducks flying over the lake, and I stood for a long time at the end of the dock and followed them with my eyes. Then Corey called me, and I ran back into the yard to play ball with him. I didn't have my leash on anymore, so he could throw the ball as far as his arm could make it go. Wherever he threw it, I would run after it and bring it back to him. I wanted Corey to throw it in the water just to see what would happen. But he was careful never to do that. He was as nervous about the water as I was. Maybe even more so.

That night, I ate food from my bowl in the same room as the pack ate their food. I slept on the floor next to the boy's bed just the way I used to sleep next to Skinny Man. The next morning when I woke up—oh, joy!—they let me out into the backyard to piddle while the scents of the night still clung to the trees and the bushes and the grass. There is nothing quite as satisfying as an early-morning piddle in the dewy morning air. I pooped, too, and Corey said, "Good girl!" and scooped it up instead of making faces the way Bad Dog Walker had.

As if all this weren't quite wonderful enough, when I went back inside, there was *more* food in my bowl. I was going to like this new home, even if they still wouldn't let me into the room where the cat was. Sometimes I smelled Cat on the boy's hands and I had to wonder what was so special about this cat.

Then one day, I walked past that door and saw that it was wide open! Corey and his mother were standing there. They both watched me as I poked my nose in the open door.

"It's okay, girl," Corey said to me. "We think

Buttercup is finally ready to meet you."

Standing in the middle of the room was the tiniest little kitten I had ever seen. She opened her mouth wide and squeezed out a tiny little *mew*. I stretched out my front legs and bent down with my muzzle on my paws and my rear end in the air, wagging. *You're cute! Want to play?* I said.

Her back went up and she hissed. *Stay away from me!* For such a little thing, she had a lot of pluck, I'll give her that.

Corey sat down on the floor and put the kitten on his lap. He stroked her until she began to purr. It was a sound I had never heard before. It was a nice warm sound, that purr. It made me want to curl up beside her and take a nap.

"It's okay, Buttercup," Corey said in a soothing voice. "I know I told you I'd bring home a kitty friend for you, but I got us a doggie friend instead.

Her name is Ginger. Ginger wants to be friends with you. She's even the same color as you."

Corey reached out his free hand to me. "Come meet Buttercup, Ginger. Buttercup, be nice to my new dog and don't scratch her, do you hear? She's already got one scar. Let's not give her another."

I scooted along the floor very slowly toward the kitten, making myself as small and meek as possible. The kitty was little, but I knew cats had sharp claws. I remembered the face full of claws I had gotten from my run-in with the raccoon. Never again! So when the kitty stopped purring, I froze. Then she climbed out of the boy's lap and stepped toward me on her tiny, delicate paws. Her tail was standing stiffly up in the air. She started purring again as she rubbed herself against my side. I lay there quietly and let her walk all around me, rubbing and purring. I kept myself very still. When she came back to my head, she nuzzled my muzzle.

"*Awww.* I think Ginger may have found a new friend," said Corey's Mother, who was still watching from the doorway.

That kitten really needed me. For one thing, she was dirty. *You're a cat,* I told her. *You're supposed to be clean. This is how you do it.* I started to lick her all over.

"Look! Ginger is cleaning Buttercup, just like a mother cat."

Thanks, Big Gal, Buttercup said to me in her teeny-tiny voice. *I needed that.*

After a few days of my doing this, Buttercup got the idea. Her little pink tongue darted out and she started to clean herself all over, from the tip of her tail to the end of her nose. She was very thorough. She did a much better job of it than I ever did, and I have to admit she smelled better. She smelled like Sunshine and Clean Clothes.

Buttercup and I became fast friends. She was allowed to sleep in the bed with the boy. But sometimes in the middle of the night, if Corey was too restless, she would jump down and sleep with me, curled up against my head. It felt pretty nice.

In the daytime, she followed me everywhere. *Where to now, Big Gal?* she'd ask.

Buttercup was good company for me when the boy went away, which he did almost every day. While he was gone, Corey's Mother would let me out in the yard to do my business or to run around and Play. Every time I went outside, Buttercup stood by the door and tried to slip out.

Nothing doing, Small Stuff, I told her. *Kittens who go outside don't last nearly as long as kittens who stick to the indoors. That's what my friend Bruce tells people who come to him for cats.* For good measure, I told her about Raccoons and Hawks and Trucks.

I get the message, she said. She shrank back and settled for watching me from the window.

One day, while I was nosing around after chipmunks, I discovered something in the side yard. Some other dog, a long time ago, had dug a hole underneath the fence. I wriggled through the hole to the other side. And what do you think I found there? Another yard just like mine, except this one had a little girl standing in it.

She ran up to me and knelt down and looked at the tag on my collar. "Hey, Ginger!" she said. "Want to play?"

Did I ever! She didn't have a ball, but who needed a ball when there was a world full of sticks? She threw a stick. I chased after it and brought it back to her. It was a simple game, but it was loads of fun. Sometimes I'd lie down and chew on the stick until she grabbed it away from me and threw it again. And then she threw the stick into the water. I paused for just a moment. Then I jumped into the water after it. For a moment, I treaded water with my nose in the air. I felt so much lighter in the lake. The water was cold and tingly. I lapped at it. It tasted delicious, like Fish and Wood and Leaves. And then I started to swim. Who knew I could swim? But now that I had started, I never wanted to stop. Then I remembered the stick. I needed to retrieve that stick for my new friend. I stopped swimming and looked around. The stick was bobbing in the water some distance away. Even

in the lake, I'd know that stick anywhere. Swimming over to it, I clamped it in my jaws and gave it a good chew. Then I swam back to shore and brought the stick to the girl. She clapped her hands and said, "Good dog!"

Have I told you how much I love hearing those two words?

I shook myself from head to tail, throwing the water off my coat. She laughed and wiped her face

on her sleeve and said, "Thanks for the shower, Ginger!" Then she threw the stick back into the water.

Yippee! I leapt back in. I loved swimming. Who knew anything in the world could be this much fun?

Then I heard Corey calling my name. He sounded worried, so I dropped the stick and said to the girl, *Gotta go. It's been fun, but my boy is calling me. See you later.*

I wriggled back under the fence. When Corey saw me, he ran over and hugged me. "Where *were* you, girl? I was worried sick about you. And— *yuck!*—you're all wet!"

"She was over here, with me," said the girl from the other side of the fence. "I'm Emma."

"Nobody told me there was a kid living next door," Corey said, standing up. For a moment, he was so interested in the girl, he forgot all about me.

"I don't live here exactly. My grammy does. But I come here after school because my parents work. Did you just move in? What's your name?"

"Corey," the boy said. "We moved in three weeks ago."

Emma said, "You're lucky. Ginger's a great dog. I love golden retrievers. I want one so bad but my folks say dogs are too messy and more responsibility than I can handle at my age."

"How old are you?" Corey asked.

"Nine," said Emma.

"*I'm* nine and I handle it fine. Ginger seems to like you a lot. My dad says retrievers love water, but she never went in the lake for me," Corey said.

The girl shrugged her shoulders. "I just went out on the dock and threw a stick in the water. She dived in right after it and brought it back to me, just like a retriever's supposed to do."

"Wow," said the boy. "I wish she'd do that for me, but I'm not allowed out on my dock."

"How come?" the girl asked.

"Because I can't swim," said Corey. "I'm supposed to take lessons this summer. Maybe then I'll be able to go out on the dock. Do you want to come over and play sometime?"

She did. After that, Emma came over almost every day to play with Corey and me and Buttercup. Sometimes Buttercup and I just lay with them on the floor while they watched a big flickering box full of light and noise. Other times, they would teach me tricks. They taught me Sit and Lie Down and Roll Over and Shake Hands. It was a good way to get treats in between meals and it seemed to make them very happy. Other times, we'd go outside and play ball or, my favorite, Fetch the Stick.

I kept waiting for them to throw the stick in the water so I could go swimming again, but they never did.

One warm day, Corey and Emma built a den in the backyard and called it a Tent. They played in the Tent all day. I was surprised when they brought me out after dinner to sleep in the Tent. Was this some sort of new game? Or was this where we were going to sleep from now on? I hoped not. It was scary in the Tent at night. There were all sorts of rustling sounds and smells I didn't recognize. I cuddled up between Corey and Emma, hoping they would protect me.

"My grammy says there are wolverines in the area," said Emma in a low, shaking voice.

"Go see if there's a wolverine out there, Ginger," Corey said. He pushed me toward the mouth of the Tent.

I whimpered. I didn't want to leave. It felt safe in here and dangerous out there. For all I knew that thing making the rustling noise might be the raccoon with sharp claws, coming back to give me another swipe across the muzzle.

"Don't you want to be our watchdog, Ginger?" Emma said to me.

I burrowed down to the bottom of the big, soft bag Corey was sleeping in. *No!*

I heard the two kids laughing softly. "Ginger can play ball and do tricks, but I don't think she's a very good watchdog," said Emma.

"Yeah, but she makes an excellent foot warmer," said Corey.

I stayed in the bottom of the big, soft bag next to Corey's feet until I heard the first morning birds call me outside to piddle. Now that the sun was shining again, I was grateful that we had survived the night, and I was ready for Play all day.

Then one day, after a storm, it was very windy. Corey tossed the stick. He had a pretty strong arm but I guess the wind was stronger, because it grabbed the stick and carried it out over the lake. Finally! I ran out to the end of the dock and leapt into the water. I looked around, treading water. Where was that stick? Unlike the other time I had gone swimming, the lakewater was murky and choppy today. I looked everywhere but I couldn't see it. I saw all kinds of sticks floating in the water but none of them was *my* stick.

Somewhere behind me, I heard Corey and Emma shouting to me but I didn't pay them any mind. I had to find that stick. Then Corey ran out to the end of the dock. He was jumping up and down and shouting and pointing. I looked to where he was pointing. Then I ducked under the water. *There* was my stick! It had sunk nearly to the muddy lake bottom. I swam down to it, fastened my mouth around it, and swam back up to the surface.

Ta-da! But just as my head broke the surface, Corey wobbled and fell into the lake with me.

New game, I thought. It was called Splashing and Gasping. But then something told me this wasn't a game. Corey's eyes were wide open and more scared than I had ever seen them. And the way he was moving his arms was wrong! I swam over to him just as he sank under the water. I dived down and placed my body between him and the lake bottom. When I swam back up to the surface, I brought him with me. Corey kept flailing and it was difficult to stay beneath him. If he wasn't careful, he was going to slip away from me and sink under the water again, just like my stick.

"Grab on to Ginger!" Emma shouted from the dock. "Grab on to the dog!"

Corey stopped thrashing. He reached out and wrapped his arms around my neck. He held me almost too tightly, but that was okay. My legs were still free to swim. And swim they did, all four of them churning, bringing us both back to the shore.

FRED AND GINGER

By the time we reached the shore, Corey's Mother had burst out of the house and run down to the lakeside. From next door, Emma's grammy had run out onto her dock. Everybody was shouting and crying. I didn't understand what the fuss was about. I was fine. Corey seemed fine, too, although he was wet and coughing and sobbing. I stepped away from him to shake the water from my coat. Then I went back and licked his face to try to bring him back to his old self. His face tasted nice and salty.

"Thank you, Ginger," Corey said to me, wrapping his arms around my neck again, only much more gently this time. "You saved my life."

I don't know what he was talking about, but I was very happy the game was over.

That night, Corey's Father gave me a bone bigger than my head to chew on.

What a great treat! What a great pack! What a wonderful new home I had found!

After that, we didn't play Splashing and Gasping again. Corey spent more time away from me than he ever had before. I had to admit, it worried me a little. Would he go away and never come back? I tried to keep myself busy with the brand-new toys his father and mother had given me. And there was always Buttercup. Buttercup learned to play Floor Ball with me. It was fun, but it wasn't as much fun as playing ball with Corey. When my boy came back at night, he was too tired to play. But he hugged me extra hard and he told me about his day.

"Guess where I've been, Ginger," he said. "I've been taking swimming lessons at the town pool."

What was a town pool? All I knew was that he tasted terrible! I had to lick his entire face to get back his regular flavor.

"Do you know what stroke I can do, Ginger?" he asked. "I do the dog paddle. And I learned it from you!"

All I knew was that when the weather turned hot, I got a big surprise. Corey ran outside one day and jumped right in the lake. I was after him like a shot, figuring he would sink like a stick again. But this time, his head bobbed back to the surface and he laughed. He didn't need my help! He wasn't splashing or gasping. He was swimming, just like me.

Playing ball in the water was even more fun than playing ball on the land. Emma came over to swim, too. We played Three-Way Ball and Race to the Dock. We played like this every day. On hot, muggy days, there was no better place for me with my thick coat than in the cool lake.

One day, we were lying around in the shade near the lake, waiting to swim again, when Emma said to me, "Guess what tomorrow is, Ginger. Tomorrow's my birthday! I'm sorry you can't come to my party, but you know how my parents are about dogs."

The next day, I played by myself. Buttercup and I played Bat the Ball around the kitchen. The ball rolled behind the stove. I poked my nose behind there. It smelled mysterious and delicious, like a thousand crumbs of People Food. But I couldn't reach that ball. Buttercup won the game because she folded herself up small enough to squeeze behind the stove and get the ball. How do cats *do* that?

When Corey finally came home to me, Emma was with him. And someone else was there, too. Another dog! Corey's Mother stood next to me with her hand hooked in my collar. Corey and Emma stood on either side of the new dog. Everyone was nervous and excited. I didn't quite understand. What was this other dog doing in my yard with my kids? The dog seemed eager and friendly enough. He had big floppy ears and a waggy tail and a golden coat just like mine.

"Ginger," Emma said, "I have someone I want you to meet. When my parents heard about you saving Corey's life, they decided to let me have a dog. They took me to Bruce's and I found my very own golden retriever. This one's a boy. His previous owner called him Red, but since I'm hoping he'll be your new friend, I want to call him Fred. My parents told me there was this famous old-time movie dance team called Ginger Rogers and Fred Astaire. You guys can be Fred and Ginger! What do you think, Ginger? Is Fred a good name for my new dog and your new doggie dance partner?"

I walked up slowly and sniffed at this new dog. He stood still and let me have a good whiff of him. I couldn't help but feel that there was something mighty familiar about this dog. Maybe it was the ears. Maybe it was his scent. Could this possibly be my long-lost brother Floppy Ears?

By any chance does Cage Nine mean anything to you? I asked him.

Fred's floppy ears practically flipped. *Of course! You're Puppy Number One of Six!* he said. *I thought you smelled familiar! What have you been doing with yourself?*

I let Floppy Ears or Red or Fred—whatever his name was, he was my brother—take his turn sniffing at me. I told him about all the places I'd been since leaving the pet shop. I told him about Dylan, and Alice the nice animal-control lady. I told him about Skinny Man and Whitey and Spotty, about Snaggletooth and Shaggy and Yappy, about Bruce and Elka and more vets than you can shake a stick at. He was impressed.

All this time, I've just had one home, Fred told me. *It was a good home, but my girl went away to something called College, and I went to Bruce's. So now I got myself a new girl. And a new name that sounds enough like my old one to make me come running when I'm called. So far, so good.*

Oh, you'll like Emma, I told Fred. *Wait'll she takes you swimming in the lake.*

"Fred, show Ginger all the tricks you know," said Emma. "Ginger, Fred knows almost as many tricks as you do."

I didn't know what she was talking about, but I went up to my brother and said, *Oh, yeah?* as I grabbed his floppy ear in my mouth and tugged

with all my might. Fred turned around and boxed
me with his paw.

Yeah! he said.

I clamped my mouth over his muzzle. He
shook me off and fastened his muzzle over mine.

And then we were at it, just like old times, all ears and tails, rolling around and tussling and yapping and having a fine old time.

"Oh, no!" said Emma, running back and forth in front of us. "We have to do something. They're fighting!"

"No, they're not," said Corey's Mother. "They're playing."

"They're not playing," said Corey. "Can't you tell? Fred and Ginger are *dancing*!"

I don't think I have ever known such happiness. We dogs like to say that the next best thing to finding a *furever* family is finding a furry playmate. And now I was one golden retriever who had found it all! Not bad for Puppy One of Six from Cage Nine, wouldn't you say? Not bad at all.

APPENDIX

More About the Golden Retriever

Golden Retrievers in History

The golden retriever was first bred in Scotland in the late 1800s on the country estate of Sir Dudley Marjoribanks (later known as Lord Tweedmouth). Sir Dudley wanted the ultimate hunting dog: a dog smart enough to find birds shot down by hunters in the field, strong enough to weather rough terrain, and gentle enough to return the birds to the hunters without crushing the bodies. The breeding of a yellow wavy-coated retriever with the now-extinct tweed water spaniel eventually led to what we know today as the golden retriever, a dog that excels at hunting, tracking, retrieving, and doing tricks. Goldens have a water-repellent coat, which comes in handy since they love to swim. The American Kennel Club first recognized the breed in 1925.

Golden Retrievers Today

Now one of the most popular breeds in America, golden retrievers are considered great family dogs because they are charming, outgoing, and good with children. Like Ginger, they are eager to please their human companions, which makes them ideal subjects for training. Goldens should be groomed regularly with a stiff brush to reach their undercoat and given ample daily exercise. Goldens that are cooped up all day and not given enough exercise can get into mischief. Poor breeding has caused some goldens to suffer from something called hip dysplasia. This is a broad term that has to do with the breed's genetic tendency toward weak or loose ball-and-socket joints in their hips. Some experts feel that this is aggravated in puppy mills, where the pups are kept in cages with wire floors and are fed high-calorie food that causes them to grow too quickly.

Puppy Mills

There are thousands of puppy mills in America. Puppy mills are businesses that turn out puppies as products and place the profitability of selling them over the welfare of the puppies and the dogs that breed them. Like chickens in crates laying eggs, bitches—or female dogs—in puppy mills spend their entire lives in wire cages, where they are forced to whelp—or give birth to—one litter after another. Neither mothers nor their puppies get toys, exercise, or the warmth and love of a human family. The reason why puppy mills continue to thrive is that many people seem to prefer purebred puppies to mixed-breed puppies, or mutts. It is also cheaper for pet stores to buy their puppies from puppy mills than from breeders. Most breeders will not sell their puppies to pet stores. They would much rather sell directly to the pet owners. That way, they can ensure that their puppies go to responsible, caring families. What is the best way to rid the world of puppy mills? Don't buy puppies from pet stores. Buy puppies from breeders if you must, but be prepared to spend hundreds, sometimes even thousands of dollars for a purebred golden retriever puppy. Even better, you might want to consider adopting a dog from a shelter.

To find a reputable breeder of golden retrievers in your area, contact the Golden Retriever Club of America:

grca.org/allabout/puppyreferrals.html

Rescue Groups

There are rescue groups for almost all existing breeds of dogs, and many of them specialize in golden retrievers. Like Ginger, sometimes goldens go to the wrong homes. Either the human companions are away too much and don't give the dog enough company and exercise or, like Dylan's parents, they underestimate the commitment and hard work that having a pet represents.

To find a golden retriever rescue group in your

area, you can contact the Golden Retriever Club of America National Rescue Committee:

grca-nrc.org

To find rescue groups for other dog breeds, check out the American Kennel Club:

akc.org/breeds/rescue.cfm

Animal Control or Animal Shelters

There are not-for-profit organizations that work to find homes for homeless or abandoned animals. They also protect members of the human community from stray animals or animals whose owners are irresponsible. Animal shelters are staffed by a combination of paid and volunteer workers. The workers clean out cages and runs, care for the animals, and work with people who are giving up their pets or looking to adopt. Unfortunately, there are more unwanted animals than most shelters can handle. Animals that have not been adopted after many weeks, or animals that have been repeatedly returned, often have to be put down so that room can be made for new animals. There are, however, some shelters that are called no-kill facilities. You can support your local animal shelter by donating food and money, and, with your parents' permission, volunteering to help socialize or walk the dogs. And of course, if you choose to get a dog of your own, you can adopt from a shelter. There are many great dogs in shelters that need homes.

To find an animal shelter in your area, visit:

aspca.org/findashelter

petfinder.com/shelters.html

The following site provides a state-by-state

listing of shelters whose policy is not to put animals down:

nokillnetwork.org

The official websites of the American Society for the Prevention of Cruelty to Animals and the Humane Society of the United States offer lots of good information on adoption, pet care, and how you can prevent animal cruelty:

aspca.org

humanesociety.org

How to Pick a Dog

Here are some steps you can take to give yourself a leg up on finding a friendly, sociable dog at a shelter:

Ask about the shelter's return policy. A good shelter will always take a dog back if, for whatever reason, you are unable to keep him or her.

Ask the shelter if you are allowed to visit with the dog outside of the kennel. If that's not allowed, this is not a shelter you want to deal with.

Ask the shelter if they screen dogs for disease or behavior problems. You don't want to adopt a sick dog or one that has a bad history. These animals need homes, too, but they are best placed with people who have experience caring for animals with problems, like our hero, Bruce!

Try not to decide in advance what kind of dog you want. Keep an open mind. But also keep in mind the size of your house and yard. And if you or someone in your family is allergic, your family should meet several dogs to see if they cause a problem because of their saliva or hair dander. The effect can vary from breed to breed and from dog to dog. Sometimes pollen on the dog's coat is what makes people sneeze, and the dog gets blamed by mistake.

If you see a dog that catches your eye, stop and visit her. Put a hand up to the cage. If the dog is friendly, she should come up and sniff your hand. If the dog sniffs your hand and wags her tail, ask if you can visit with the dog outside the cage in a quiet area.

Be with the dog for five minutes and ignore her. If she shows no interest in making friends with you, put her back. If she's friendly, pet her. She should enjoy being stroked and should lean into you. If she shakes you off or moves away, she's telling you she isn't interested in making friends.

If she continues to be friendly, bring out a toy—a ball or a piece of rope. Play fetch or tug-of-war for a few minutes. Then stop playing and put the toy out of sight. If the dog growls or takes too long to settle down after playing, she might be too excitable.

Ask if you can leash the dog and take her for a walk. See if you can take her past people of different sizes and shapes. If she doesn't bark at people and the things she sees, that's another sign that you've found yourself a good dog.

Of course, there is no guarantee that the dog you find anywhere, much less at a shelter, will work out for you. But it helps to start out with a few advantages, like health and a friendly, easygoing disposition. Good luck, if and when the time comes, finding your furever friend.